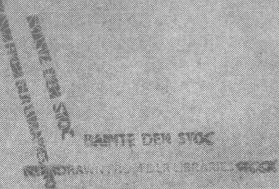

THE HOLIDAYS

GECKO PRESS

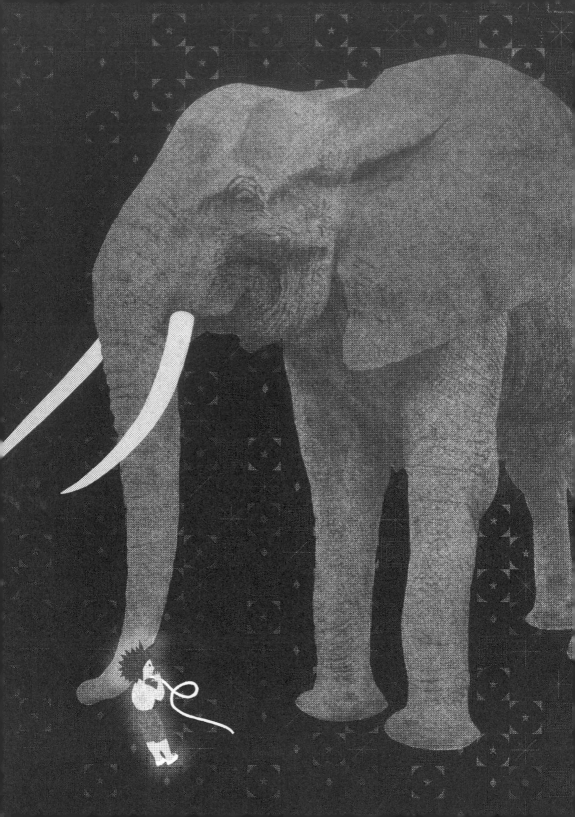

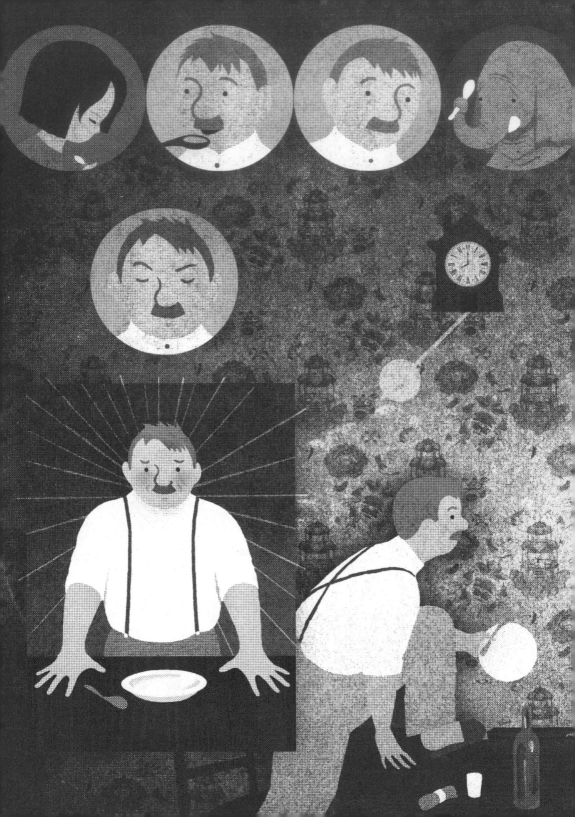

XXXXXX

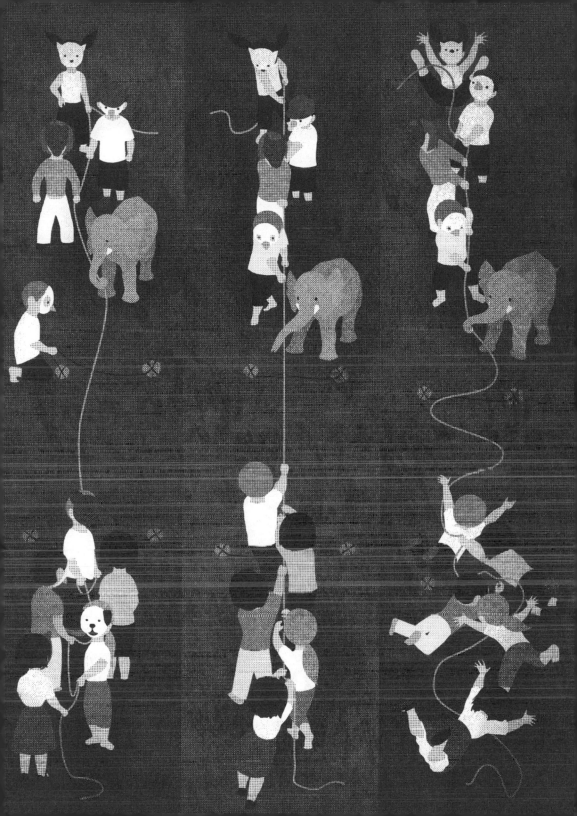

This edition first published in 2018 by Gecko Press

PO Box 9335, Wellington 6141, New Zealand / info@geckopress.com

© Gecko Press Ltd 2018

Original title: Nos Vacances © 2017 Albin Michel Jeunesse

Distributed in the United Kingdom by Bounce Sales and Marketing, bouncemarketing.co.uk

Distributed in Australia by Scholastic Australia, scholastic.com.au

Distributed in New Zealand by Upstart Distribution, upstartpress.co.nz

Typesetting by Spencer Levine / Printed in China

For more curiously good books, visit geckopress.com